Zach and Lucy

and the
Museum of
Natural Wonders

By the Pifferson Sisters
Illustrated by Mark Chambers

Ready-to-Read

Simon Spotlight
New York   London   Toronto   Sydney   New Delhi

SIMON SPOTLIGHT
An imprint of Simon & Schuster Children's Publishing Division
1230 Avenue of the Americas, New York, New York 10020
This Simon Spotlight edition January 2016

For information about special discounts for bulk purchases, please contact Simon & Schuster
Special Sales at 1-866-506-1949 or business@simonandschuster.com.
Manufactured in the United States of America 1215 LAK
2 4 6 8 10 9 7 5 3 1
Library of Congress Cataloging-in-Publication Data
Pifferson Sisters. Zach and Lucy and the museum of natural wonders / by the Pifferson
Sisters ; illustrated by Mark Chambers. pages cm. — (Ready-to-read)
ISBN 978-1-4814-3935-0 (trade pbk. : alk. paper) — ISBN 978-1-4814-3936-7 (hardcover : alk.
paper) — ISBN 978-1-4814-3937-4 (eBook)
[1. Museums—Fiction. 2. Brothers and sisters—Fiction. 3. Apartment houses—Fiction.
4. Behavior—Fiction. 5. Humorous stories.]
I. Chambers, Mark, 1980- illustrator. II. Title.
PZ7.1.P54Zah 2016
[Fic]—dc23
2014049369

CONTENTS

CHAPTER 1:
Lucy's Big Idea

Lucy and Zach live in apartment 2B in the Royal Amherst Building.

Lucy is the older sister, and she likes to make things up.

Zach is the younger brother, and he likes to make things happen.

They stay out of trouble—most of the time.

The Royal Amherst Building is a tall,
old brick building with many hiding spots,
an elevator that sometimes works, and a
doorman named Ned. It has a garden on
the roof and a very dark basement.

It's in a big city, on a busy street full of
stores, people, and parks.

Lucy and Zach can go almost anywhere
on the block, as long as they stay together.

Lucy and Zach think their neighborhood is perfect for all sorts of things.

Some think it was perfect before Lucy and Zach got there.

One morning, Lucy and Zach looked at a book from the Museum of Natural History.

"Zach," said Lucy, "everything in this museum comes from outdoors."

"Yes," said Zach.

"We go outdoors."

"True," said Zach.

"We could make a museum!" said Lucy.

"Are you sure about that?" asked Zach.

"Trust me," said Lucy.

CHAPTER 2:
Collectors

Zach already had his moss collection.
But it takes more than moss to make a
museum!

"Let's hunt for specimens," said Lucy.

"What are specimens?" asked Zach.

"It's the stuff in museums you can't
touch."

"Oh," said Zach. "But where will we
put them?"

"In my backpack," said Lucy.

"They might get broken," said Zach.
"Wait a minute."

11

"Where did you get those boxes?" asked Lucy.

"Mom's closet," said Zach. "Don't worry. I took out the jewelry."

"Mom, can we go look for things for our museum?" asked Zach and Lucy.

"Yes," said Mom. "Remember the rules.
Stay together, stay on the block . . ."

"And don't bother Mrs. Blankenship,"
finished Zach and Lucy.

Lucy and Zach said good-bye to Ned, who was in charge of the door, the keys, the basement, and lots of other important things.

Then they began their hunt. They had to decide which specimens to keep . . .

. . . and which to leave alone.

By the end, they'd collected some rabbit droppings, one egg, one branch shaped like a hand, one pretty rock, one ugly rock, one thing that might be an arrowhead, two kinds of moss Zach didn't have, one thing that might be an owl pellet, one mushroom, and one dead centipede.

CHAPTER 3:
Borrowers

"We still don't have enough for a real museum," said Lucy.

"Maybe we could borrow Oliver's tarantula," suggested Zach.

On the way to see Oliver in apartment 2D, Zach and Lucy passed by Ned.

"Ned, do you have anything you could lend us for our museum of natural wonders?" asked Lucy.

"Well . . . ," said Ned, "I don't think so."

Zach and Lucy went to every floor of the
Royal Amherst Building.

Oliver loaned his tarantula.

Lisa in 3F loaned two starfish from her
bathroom.

Henry in 4H loaned his baby teeth.

Sydney in 5A loaned her stuffed
parakeet.

Mrs. Finney in 2E had just cleaned out
her closets. She gave them a fancy-looking
fan made out of real peacock feathers. She
even said they could keep it.

Mrs. Blankenship in 2C did not give them anything. "I sometimes wonder if children should be allowed inside museums," said Mrs. Blankenship. She closed the door firmly.

CHAPTER 4:
The Perfect Place

The basement of the Royal Amherst Building was dark. It was mysterious. It was a big, empty, mysterious, dark place with no grown-ups. It was perfect.

Zach moved some boxes.
Lucy decorated the boxes.
Zach set up the lighting.
Lucy decorated the lighting.
Zach cut some cardboard to make a sign.
Lucy decorated the sign.

Soon the museum was ready to open.

"Ned," said Zach, "will you come to
our museum of natural wonders in the
basement?"

"Can't wait!" said Ned.

Lucy knocked on doors. "There's a special exhibit in the basement. One day only. It's free, but donations are welcome."

"Natural wonders," said Lucy. "Right in the basement."

"A real museum," said Lucy, "with strange creatures from around the world."

Naturally, people were curious.

Some might say worried.

Lucy wasn't planning to invite Mrs. Blankenship, because she did not think Mrs. Blankenship would want to come. But Mrs. Blankenship heard Lucy inviting her next-door neighbor, and she decided to go anyway.

Mrs. Blankenship had a suspicion that the children were

UP
TO
NO
GOOD.

27

CHAPTER 5:
The Grand Opening

Mrs. Blankenship took the elevator to the basement. She was first in line.

Zach politely said nothing when Mrs. Blankenship did not offer a donation.

"Welcome to the Museum of Natural Wonders," said Lucy.

Zach turned on the lights.

"Don't worry, Mrs. Blankenship, that's just rabbit poop," said Zach.

"What is it doing in my basement?" gasped Mrs. Blankenship.

"It's a natural wonder," explained Lucy.

"What is that *creature*?"

"That's only Bob," said Lucy. "He's not alive . . . anymore."

Mrs. Blankenship frowned at the parakeet. She scowled at the starfish. She glared at the arrowhead.

But when Mrs. Blankenship saw the peacock feather fan, she stopped frowning. "Lovely colors," she remarked.

"It's a fan! Mrs. Finney gave it to us," said Lucy.

"It's so elegant," said Mrs. Blankenship, picking it up and holding it to her cheek.

"You look fancy," said Zach.

Mrs. Blankenship's lips moved up. Not exactly a smile. But close enough that she adjusted the fan so the children wouldn't see.

"You can have it if you want," said Zach, "after we're done with the museum."

"Well, if I can help by taking if off your hands . . . ," said Mrs. Blankenship.

CHAPTER 6:
A Secret Wonder

There were lots of great donations to the museum.

After everyone left, Ned helped Zach and Lucy clean up.

"There's one more natural wonder in the Royal Amherst," said Ned. "Would you like to see it?"

"Yes!" said Lucy.

"What kind of natural wonder?" asked Zach.

Ned put his finger to his lips.

Lucy and Zach stared in amazement.
This wonder was the most wonderful of all.

"It's a spring exhibit," said Ned. "It
comes back every year."

THE END